THE TRULY TERRIBLE MISTAKE

MORE RULES FOR
PERFECTION
(ALMOST)!

Project Best Friend
Private List for Camp Success
Lucky Jars & Broken Promises

PENELOPE PERFECT

THE TRULY
TERRIBLE MISTAKE

Chrissie Perry

J
per
#4

ALADDIN

NEW YORK LONDON TORONTO SYDNEY NEW DELHI

✨ ALADDIN
An imprint of Simon & Schuster Children's Publishing Division
1230 Avenue of the Americas, New York, New York 10020
First Aladdin paperback edition April 2018
Text copyright © 2016 by Chrissie Perry
Cover illustration copyright © 2018 by Marta Kissi
Interior illustrations copyright © 2016 by Hardie Grant Egmont
Originally published in Australia in 2016 by Hardie Grant Egmont
Published by arrangement with Hardie Grant Egmont
All rights reserved, including the right of reproduction in whole or in part in any form.
Also available in an Aladdin hardcover edition.
ALADDIN and related logo are registered trademarks of
Simon & Schuster, Inc.
For information about special discounts for bulk purchases, please contact Simon & Schuster Special Sales at 1-866-506-1949 or business@simonandschuster.com.
The Simon & Schuster Speakers Bureau can bring authors to your live event. For more information or to book an event contact the Simon & Schuster Speakers Bureau at 1-866-248-3049 or visit our website at www.simonspeakers.com.
Book designed by Laura Lyn DiSiena
The text of this book was set in Aldine 401 BT Std.
Manufactured in the United States of America 0318 OFF
10 9 8 7 6 5 4 3 2 1
Library of Congress Control Number 2017958978
ISBN 978-1-4814-9085-6 (hc)
ISBN 978-1-4814-9084-9 (pbk)
ISBN 978-1-4814-9086-3 (eBook)

THE TRULY
TERRIBLE MISTAKE

CHAPTER

Penelope Kingston loved getting report cards. She adored seeing all her excellent grades lined up in a row. They were proof of how well she was doing at school. Penelope always sent a copy to her dad, who lived in another city. He paid her twenty dollars for every A. This meant that at the end of each term, Penelope was EXTREMELY happy with herself. ⁻She was also quite rich. ⁻

Of course, it was necessary to get good

grades all through the year so she could keep enjoying excellent report cards. So, at school on Monday morning, Penelope was excited as she waited for the results of her latest math test. To tell the truth (and Penelope always told the truth), she had found the test very easy. In fact, she was hoping for a ⁻ perfect ⁻ score.

Ms. Pike was trying to get around the classroom to hand the tests back to each student. While she did that, everyone was supposed to be getting on with some English comprehension questions. Unfortunately, neither of these things was going smoothly. That was because of Joanna (the naughtiest girl in the class).

Joanna was scrunching up pieces of paper into little balls, LICKING them, putting them inside an empty pen casing, and blowing them across the classroom. So far, she'd hit two live targets. On the other side of the room, Felix

Unger rubbed the back of his neck, and Tilly flicked a slobber ball off her jumper.

Ms. Pike paused and looked around, her eyes narrowed. Penelope (who was very good at deducing) figured that Ms. Pike suspected it was Joanna. But Ms. Pike was too kind and fair to accuse her without actual evidence.

As Ms. Pike leaned down to talk to Tommy Stratton about his results, Joanna launched two more missiles. Ms. Pike paused AGAIN. At this rate, it would take her half a day to get around the classroom!

Luckily, Penelope was sitting opposite Joanna and had actual evidence that she was guilty. Penelope was (quite) sure that Ms. Pike had put Joanna on her table so Penelope could influence Joanna's BAD behavior with her own ⁻ GOOD ⁻ behavior. It was quite a big responsibility, but Penelope didn't mind.

"Joanna, you need to put that weapon down right now," Penelope said in a loud whisper. She said it in a whisper because she didn't want the other kids to think she was tattling. She made the whisper loud, though, in the hope that Ms. Pike would hear her. Sometimes Ms. Pike didn't notice Penelope helping. This time was (unfortunately) no different.

"Hang on, will you, Penelope," Joanna said, as though she was doing absolutely nothing wrong.

She licked two more balls of paper. Joanna often poked her tongue out, so Penelope had seen it far too many times. If she had to (though she could not think of a circumstance where she *would* have to), Penelope could probably describe Joanna's tongue in great detail.

"I've only got two more pellets I need to shoot."

"You actually don't *need* to shoot *any* more

pellets, Joanna," Penelope said in another (louder) whisper. "In fact, you *could* stop right now, before you get into trouble and before someone gets hurt."

Penelope thought it was a very convincing and logical argument. So when her best friend, Bob, opened her mouth to speak, Penelope was sure Bob was going to back her up.

"You know, Jo," Bob began, leaning in toward Joanna, "you're not doing it right. You've gotta use more spit and roll the balls up tighter. Then they'll fly farther and faster."

"WHOOSH!"

As she made the whooshing sound, Bob drew her hand up in the air like a rocket launching.

Penelope huffed. Even though Bob's advice was correct, it was not Good Advice. Unfortunately Bob didn't see her huff because she was leaning in toward Joanna. Penelope tugged her arm so she would sit back.

"Stop encouraging Joanna, Bob," Penelope whispered.

Bob screwed up her nose. One of the interesting things about having her very own best friend was that Penelope could often tell what Bob was about to say, based on the faces she made. Bob screwing up her nose, for instance, made Penelope suspect that she was about to disagree with her.

"I'm not exactly encouraging Joanna, Pen," Bob said. "I'm just saying if she's going to do it, then she could do it a lot better."

In a weird way, it was actually quite satisfying that Penelope's prediction was correct. It meant that Penelope really understood her best friend.

Bob was the most terrific best friend ever. Even though she sometimes saw things differently from Penelope, most of the time Penelope didn't mind. Because Bob always told Penelope the truth about what she was thinking, and that was a Very Important Thing in a best friend.

Penelope reached over to confiscate Joanna's pen so that she could convince Bob without being distracted. She did not confiscate the slobber balls, since that would have meant touching them. Without the pen they were useless anyway.

"Well, teaching Joanna how to do it better actually *is* encouraging her," Penelope told her best friend.

"Nah," Bob argued (she could be very stubborn!). "I think Joanna would shoot those pellets anyway."

Normally, Penelope would have kept trying to explain why she was right, but this time she didn't.

Because Ms. Pike was (finally) walking toward their table with the pile of tests.

☺ ☺ ☺

"You did really well," Ms. Pike said as she handed Joanna her test. "You should be very proud of yourself."

As Joanna held up her test and beamed, Ms. Pike snuck Penelope one of her small but lovely smiles. Near the beginning of the year, when Joanna was struggling with math, Penelope had volunteered to coach her for half an hour a week after school. Now that Penelope had her very own best friend (and was quite a lot busier than she used to be) she sometimes wondered if it was worth giving up her time.

Sometimes, Penelope suspected (even though she always used her most calm, patient voice) that Joanna wasn't listening. One time, she actually found proof. Penelope had heard a dull, distant *doof doof* sound. She'd followed the sound, lifting up a section of Joanna's bushy hair, and discovered that she had earphones hidden underneath. That had been very upsetting. If Joanna hadn't BEGGED for another chance, insisting that her mum was going to kill her, Penelope (even though she absolutely wasn't a quitter) might have quit.

Now, she was glad she hadn't. Getting one of Ms. Pike's small but lovely smiles was very nice. Plus, Penelope loved helping people (even naughty ones). — 15/20 was Joanna's best result so far.

Penelope didn't mind that Sarah was the next person at her table to get her test back (17/20), and she was very happy for Bob (18/20). She told herself it was — POSITIVE — that she was going to be the last person in the entire class to get her test back. Ms. Pike was stretching out the excitement.

Ms. Pike's small but lovely smile seemed to turn into a frown as she handed Penelope her test, but Penelope didn't think much of it. Sometimes Ms. Pike looked like that just before recess.

Penelope shut her eyes briefly. Then she looked.

It was as though her heart was in an elevator that had suddenly plummeted fifty stories. Not literally. Literally, her heart was in the same spot, but that's not what it felt like.

Because the score on her test wasn't a perfect score.

It wasn't even a *nearly* perfect score.

"Everyone makes mistakes, Penelope," Ms. Pike said for the third time. The other students had gone out for recess.

"Please let me do it again," Penelope pleaded. She could hardly believe how Truly Terrible her mistake was. She had ENTIRELY MISSED five questions on the very back page. Five questions that she could (if she'd seen them!) have answered correctly. It was, perhaps, one of the STUPIDEST things she had ever done.

"I'll do it at lunchtime. Or after school. Please, Ms. Pike."

Ms. Pike sighed.

"I'm sorry, Penelope," she said softly. "I can't let you do the test again. If I let you do that, I'd have to let everyone do it every time they made a mistake."

"But it wasn't a *normal* mistake," Penelope pointed out. "I know how to answer those questions. I really do. This is just"—she hit her forehead with the palm of her hand—"this is just a NIGHTMARE. I got 15/20 for a Very Important Test!"

She paused to let that sink in. And then, just in case it hadn't sunk in properly, she continued. "I got the

PENELOPE IMAGINED HER DAD LOOKING AT THE TERRIBLE REPORT CARD.

same grade as *Joanna!* And it will RUIN my report card!"

"Penelope," Ms. Pike said, and now her voice wasn't as soft, "you need to learn how to cope when you don't get a perfect grade. I'm sure you won't make the same mistake again. You need to move on."

Penelope took a big breath. Before she exhaled, Bob appeared at the classroom door. Well, Bob's head appeared at the classroom door. The rest of her was probably on its way back to the playground.

"Come on, Pen," she urged. "You're going to waste the entire recess." Bob looked at Ms. Pike and giggled. "No offense, Miss," she added.

Even though Ms. Pike didn't like being called Miss, she smiled back. Bob was the kind of person who made other people smile. Even at this Truly Terrible time, Bob made Penelope feel a tiny bit better.

"No offense taken, Bob," Ms. Pike said. "Please do take Penelope out into the fresh air, or the recess will indeed be over."

Penelope sighed loudly.

"Maybe I can do an *extra* test?" she suggested.

Penelope thought it was a Good Suggestion, but Ms. Pike must have really needed her coffee, because she just shook her head and ushered Penelope out of the classroom.

CHAPTER

2

By the time Penelope got home that afternoon, she knew there was nothing she could do about the math test. It was a Very Sad thing to know.

Her big brother, Harry, had been to the dentist after chipping a tooth at soccer, so he was home early. You'd think a chipped tooth would have put him off soccer for a while, but he and their mum were in the front yard. Penelope's mum was tossing the soccer ball and Harry was butting it with his head. It looked ridiculous. *No hands* was a silly soccer rule, if you asked Penelope. Which no one ever did.

"Hey, Poss, how was your day?" her mum asked. Harry headbutted the ball and it flew past Penelope's face, just missing her.

"TERRIBLE," Penelope answered. "My day was terrible."

Her mum caught the ball and held on to it. Harry got an antsy look on his face and jiggled from foot to foot. Harry wasn't good at waiting for Penelope to share her news. He could be quite selfish like that.

"What happened, chook?" her mum asked.

"Well, I practically *failed* my math test."

Normally, Penelope stuck to the facts and didn't exaggerate. But her mum and Harry didn't always share Penelope's ideas about what was important, and she wanted her mum's full attention.

"Oh well," her mum said lightly. "Don't take it to heart. There's always next time."

Penelope sucked in a breath and held it.

"I fail math all the time," Harry joined in, still jiggling around. "Don't sweat it."

"There's no point even talking to you two about it," Penelope said as she walked through the front door.

Truly, sometimes it felt like Harry and her mum were from a different planet.

Penelope walked into the kitchen. She rolled her eyes when she saw the shopping on the bench. Honestly, when Harry went to the supermarket with her mum, they came home with even *more* junk food than usual.

A big packet of Assorted Cream Biscuits was right there in front of her. Penelope always tried to stick to the guidelines of the food pyramid, but there were rarely the right foods in the house. Honestly, it was no wonder she had made such a silly mistake. She was (possibly) under-nourished.

She took a Chocolate Cream biscuit from the packet. Chocolate Cream biscuits were definitely from the top layer of the food pyramid (eat rarely). But, seeing as her mum hadn't done a PROPER shop, Penelope didn't have much choice but to eat it. It was the same with the Monte Carlo and the Orange Slice.

Penelope had to admit, some things from the top of the food pyramid tasted really good. For about ten minutes, Penelope enjoyed the sugar high.

But after that faded, Penelope just felt worse than ever.

She wished she could phone her father and confess her Terrible Mistake right away (unfortunately she couldn't because he was a politician and a Very Busy Man and he had a new family now). Penelope very much liked the precious twenty dollars he gave her for each A on her school report card. But that was nowhere near as important as making him proud.

Instead (because she was allowed to do this absolutely any time she wanted) she got her iPhone and texted him.

> Hi, Dad. I had a bad day. I made a big mistake in my math test and now I won't be getting an A for math. I asked Ms. Pike if I could repeat the test and she said no. I'm sorry to disappoint you. P x

After she pressed send, Penelope ate one more Monte Carlo. But there was still a hollow feeling inside her. She kept an eye on her iPhone, but there was no reply.

The sad feeling she'd carried around with her all day started to change. The sad was still there, but on top of it (and four sweet biscuits) was an angry feeling. This wasn't entirely bad. At least the mad part of her had more energy. She marched back down the hall and threw open the front door.

"There is NOTHING healthy in that shopping, Mum!" she said, standing in the doorway with her hands on her hips. "It's just NOT responsible," she finished.

"Uh-oh," Harry replied (even though she hadn't spoken to *him*). He pointed to the space above Penelope in a gesture that was (unfortunately) quite familiar.

"Look, that little black cloud is following you around again."

Penelope glared at Harry. Ever since she was little, he'd taunted her with that silly saying.

IT WAS EXTREMELY ANNOYING.

And it didn't even make sense. Nobody had their very own cloud, black or white.

"Okay, okay, time out," her mum said. "Penelope, I've already put some of the shopping away. There's whole-grain bread in the pantry. And fruit in the bowl. And Grandpa dropped some vegetable soup over for dinner. Is that okay with you?"

"Yes," Penelope said (very graciously, she thought, given that her mum had practically **HIDDEN** all the nutritious food). "I guess that's okay."

It had been four hours and twenty-two minutes since Penelope texted her dad about her Terrible Mistake. That was a long wait, even for him. Perhaps he was so disappointed in her that he couldn't bring himself to reply. Or perhaps he was too busy trying to work out how his very own daughter could make such a silly error.

Penelope's iPhone was on the stand next to

her bed. She made sure the volume was up as high as it would go so she wouldn't miss the beep when the message came.

Her eyelids felt droopy, but she tried to stay awake. Even if her dad said he was awfully disappointed in her and not as proud as he should be, that would be better than no reply at all.

Penelope was just drifting to sleep when her phone beeped.

> Disappointing, P. Maybe u can make up for mistake in other subject? Try best. D x

The message had come at 9:47 p.m.—way after Penelope's normal bedtime. And it did wake her right up. She still felt bad about disappointing her father. But, in a way, it was a

‾POSITIVE‾ message. Her dad was right—she could make up for the grade somewhere else. Penelope was just like him really.

‾Penelope Kingston didn't get to be excellent at most things by being a quitter.‾

Tomorrow was a brand-new day. And Penelope was (quite) sure she'd be able to find a way to make up for her mistake. Surely she would be able to bring her grades up in another subject. One where there was room for improvement.

She'd just have to keep her eyes open for the right opportunity.

CHAPTER

3

On Tuesday, Penelope tried to hold on to that positive approach. She did not react when Rita (the meanest girl in the whole school) asked about her test results and then ran away laughing during Penelope's explanation. But in all the subjects Penelope had that day, there was really not much room for improvement. Which was good in a way, because it was nice to be reminded that she was still excellent at MOST things.

But it was frustrating, too.

Wednesday started off the same way. The first subjects were English and art, and Penelope was already on track to get very good grades in both.

But after recess, there was drama.

Penelope's feelings about most subjects were quite clear. She loved English, social studies, music, art, science and math. She wasn't keen on physical education. Her feelings for drama, though, were confusing. Penelope had tried to sort them out by making a list.

Good Bits About Drama
- I love scripts and I'm very good at learning lines off by heart
- I like figuring out how a character might talk and walk
- It's exciting to be in front of an audience (when I've rehearsed properly!)

Bad Bits About Drama
- *Improvisation (being stuck in front of an audience without proper preparation.!) is the worst thing EVER!*

If anyone looked at Penelope's list (which they hadn't because she had written it right near the back of her notebook, just for herself) it might seem that "Good Bits About Drama" outweighed "Bad Bits About Drama." But that would be underestimating how Penelope felt about improvisation.

If Penelope ever became a drama teacher

(which was unlikely because she was probably going to be a great politician like her dad) she would BAN improvisation.

Penelope was (quite) sure that improvisation wasn't proper drama anyway. She was more than happy to prepare for a role. She actually liked learning her lines and figuring out where to stand and how her character's voice should sound when she had a proper script to work from.

But improvisation was AWFUL. It was awful, for instance, to have to pretend (without ANY PROPER PLANNING OR PRACTICE) that you were at a rock concert and one of the band members pulled you onstage to sing into a microphone. Especially since the song was not even real and you were supposed to MAKE IT UP ON THE SPOT.

This EXACT thing had happened to

Penelope just two weeks ago. It was lucky that Oscar Finley was in her group, because when Penelope stood there in front of the WHOLE CLASS with her mouth open and her heart racing, Oscar stepped in and started playing an air guitar solo.

It was no wonder Penelope's grades for drama were sometimes (because of stupid improvisation) a little less than perfect.

Penelope crossed her fingers as she walked into drama. She'd heard rumors from other kids in her year that Mr. Salmon was giving everyone a proper, scripted project.

Penelope certainly hoped the rumors were true. Because this might be just the way to push up her drama grade and make up for her Truly Terrible Mistake.

Perhaps then her dad would stay proud of her after all.

Mr. Salmon was a very colorful teacher. His shoes were especially colorful. Penelope had kept a mental list of all the shoes he'd worn so far this year. Today's shoes were green.

"Crew, for your major assessment task, I want each group to come up with a five-minute performance," he said, walking his green shoes between the students, who all sat on the floor. "First, you will need to write your own play. The subject matter is entirely up to you."

He walked to the front of the room and checked his diary. "Now, let me see. Today is Wednesday. . . ."

Penelope tried not to count how many seconds it would take him to check his diary, but she couldn't help herself.

Eight seconds. Unfortunately, Mr. Salmon

liked to say unnecessary things before he got to the point.

"We have drama together on Wednesdays and Thursdays. So you'll have two periods after today to work on your play. Then you'll perform it in front of the class next Thursday."

As soon as Mr. Salmon said that, Penelope had a feeling that things were about to change.

For the better.

Perhaps his green shoes were good luck? Because Penelope was ready to GO with this project.

—She had found her opportunity to get an excellent grade in drama!—

Penelope felt so ENTHUSIASTIC that she sneakily reached out and pinched Bob on the thigh. It would be rude to speak while Mr. Salmon was speaking, but Penelope could hardly wait to share her good news with Bob.

SHE HAD ALREADY WRITTEN A PLAY!

Now that Penelope had her very own best friend she was always occupied (without even trying!) at lunchtimes. But before Bob came to Chelsea Primary, things had been very different. Penelope had *some* friends. Sometimes she would join Joanna and Sarah on the monkey bars, or go over to the courtyard where Tilly and Sarah were (though there was always the risk that Rita would say something very mean). Occasionally, Penelope would spend some time on the oval with Oscar Finley (even though he was a boy) while he caught bugs and examined them under his magnifying glass.

Some lunchtimes, though, Penelope didn't have anyone to play with. On those days, she'd go to the library. The Very Good Thing was that Penelope hadn't wasted those library lunchtimes. She'd put a lot of effort into writing a PLAY. She would have to wait until she was home to get it out of her special box with the lock and key and check it over again, but as far as she could remember, her play was -PERFECT.-

Penelope recalled that it even had five roles, which exactly matched the number of kids in her drama group.

Having the -EXCELLENT- play she'd

prepared earlier would give Penelope's group the biggest head start ever. While the other groups were still trying to write their scripts, Penelope's group could be learning their lines and figuring out how to talk and walk and where to stand on the stage!

Putting on a proper play wasn't silly and thoughtless like improvisation. This would take EFFORT and DISCIPLINE. Which was perfect for Penelope. She was quite sure that, with her play and her direction, her group could achieve TOP GRADES. Now there was DEFINITELY a chance of having an excellent school report card at the end of the term.

As Penelope scanned her group, preparing to deliver her great news, she caught sight of Joanna out of the corner of her eye. Joanna was practicing how to touch her nose with her tongue. Penelope knew (from past experience) the steps Joanna was going through.

1. Stretch your tongue out, making a point with the tip.
2. Pull upper lip over teeth.
3. Point tip of tongue up toward nose.

Penelope couldn't help but stare. Joanna's goal had absolutely nothing to do with drama. In fact, it was a very silly goal. Penelope would never consider putting time and energy into such a crazy thing. In that way (well, in every way actually) Joanna and Penelope were EXACT opposites.

Still, Penelope could see that Joanna was making good progress. Last time Penelope had seen her try this, Joanna's tongue had ended up at least three centimeters away from the tip of her nose. This time, the distance was probably just over one centimeter.

Penelope shook her head and tried to focus. This was the type of thing Joanna did all the time. It was EXTREMELY distracting.

By the time she focused properly, Penelope saw that Mr. Salmon was at the noticeboard.

"Okay, crew, we're going to mix it up a bit for this task," he said in a casual way, as though changing the drama group Penelope had worked with for THREE MONTHS was no big deal. "Here's a list of the brand-new groups you'll be working in."

CHAPTER

4

"It's a DISASTER!" Penelope told Bob as they walked home together that afternoon. "An absolute CATASTROPHE."

"Nah, it's not, Pen," Bob replied. "A catastrophe would be something like a tsunami. Or a cyclone. Or a volcanic eruption. Even a typhoon, or an earthquake."

As Bob reeled off her list, Penelope imagined each of the natural disasters.

"Focus, Bob," Penelope said. Bob knew a lot

EACH OF THE IMAGININGS HAD JOANNA'S FACE ON IT.

about natural disasters since she'd chosen the topic for environmental science. (Penelope had chosen pollution.)

But right now, that was not the point. "I'm talking about Joanna here. Joanna! She's the **WORST** person Mr. Salmon could ever have chosen to be in our group."

Bob shrugged. "At least we're still together, Pen."

Penelope blew out a breath. Obviously, it would have been even *worse* if Bob wasn't in her group. But clearly she didn't understand how serious this was. It was one thing to help Joanna out in math, but entirely another to have her in their drama group. This project had to make up for Penelope's Terrible Mistake in the math test.

Joanna was even NAUGHTIER (if that was possible) in drama than she was in the regular classroom. It was bad enough that they'd lost Oscar Finley (who was probably the best boy actor in the whole class) and picked up Tommy Stratton (who was an okay actor but always wanted to sing, which he was terrible at). Penelope thought she could manage Tommy Stratton. But Joanna?

"What if Joanna RUINS it for our whole group, Bob?" Penelope asked.

"What if she doesn't?" Bob said. "I mean, some of Joanna's improvisations have been awesome. And funny, too."

At the mention of improvisation, Penelope felt Very Tense.

"This is going to be a proper scripted performance, Bob," Penelope reminded her, "not just some random improvisation. Joanna gets carried away all the time."

"True that," Bob said, with a smirk that made Penelope think she was recalling one of the many times Joanna had got carried away in improvisations. "Let's just give her a chance, though, Pen. We can always pull her into line if she goes nutso."

Penelope would have liked to discuss some actual strategies for pulling Joanna into line if she went nutso, but they had arrived at Bob's house. And Bob just waved and sped up her driveway as though the whole Joanna thing was no big deal.

Whenever Penelope felt stressed or anxious (like now) she liked to see Grandpa George. When she was with Grandpa George, life always seemed a little less wobbly. And Penelope could call Grandpa George at any old time. Unlike her dad, he was hardly ever Very Busy. With Grandpa, there was always time to relax and talk about things.

‐So it was Very Good that Grandpa was able to meet Penelope for a walk in the park.‐

"Hello, sweetheart," Grandpa George said, holding up a paper bag. Penelope knew the bag would contain bread for the ducks. That was another good thing about Grandpa George. She could always rely on him to bring bread for the ducks.

Without needing to talk about it, Penelope and Grandpa George headed off toward the park. When they got there, they went straight to the lake.

"So, you've had a bit of a difficult day?" he asked. Before Penelope could answer, he continued. "It must be in the air for you Geminis. We just had another dream analysis group and Fred needed to debrief."

Grandpa George held a dream analysis group at his house once a month. There were about seven members who went. Fred was Penelope's favorite (apart from Grandpa George, of course). Fred's star sign was Gemini, just like Penelope's.

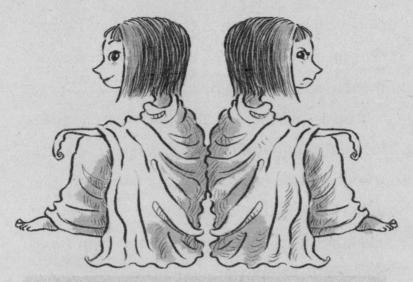

SOMETIMES, PENELOPE WASN'T SO SURE SHE LIKED BEING A GEMINI.

The sign for Gemini was of twins. Penelope wasn't a twin in actual life. In actual life, she just had Harry and her little half sister, Sienna. Even so, it often felt to Penelope that she *was* a kind of twin. It was as though there were two Penelopes inside her. One was a lovely, calm, and sensible Penelope and, thankfully, it was usually that Penelope who showed up.

But every now and then (way less than 50 percent of the time) it was the bossy, cross, and frustrated Penelope who surfaced.

Penelope didn't know many other Geminis, but she thought Grandpa's friend Fred was (possibly—she couldn't say for sure since she didn't know many others) the very best Gemini to know. Penelope had confided in Fred about the twin Penelopes, and it had been one of the smartest things she'd ever done. Because Fred totally understood.

Actually, Fred understood so well that Penelope even told him the thing she really DID NOT LIKE about being a Gemini.

Outbursts.

Occasionally (really, not very often) bad feelings would build up inside her. Then (hardly ever), the bossy, frustrated Penelope would barge right past the good, sensible, calm

Penelope. When that happened, things would fly out of her mouth. And they were NOT good things.

Penelope had been working hard on controlling her outbursts. She had lots of calming techniques, like coloring and making jewelry and reading her favorite books, which helped keep the angry Penelope away MOST of the time.

Fred used golf and lawn bowls and listening to jazz music for squashing down his not-very-nice twin. Penelope thought this was good to know for when she got old herself. Though she was (quite) sure she'd be cured of outbursts by them.

"What's up with Fred?" Penelope asked Grandpa.

"He's been having his flying dreams again," Grandpa said.

Penelope knew Fred enjoyed his flying dreams. He always said he felt as though he was getting to see the world for free.

"But his flying dreams are good, aren't they?" Penelope asked.

Grandpa George paused. "Well, the latest ones haven't been so good. He's been flying too low. It's as though he can't muster enough oomph to rise up into the air properly. So in his dreams, he keeps banging into power poles and roofs."

Penelope frowned. She didn't like the idea of Fred banging into power poles and roofs, even if it was only in his dreams.

"So, what does it mean?" Penelope asked. Grandpa George had taught her that dreams always mean *something*.

Grandpa George flattened his handlebar mustache. "It could mean that Fred has a lesson to learn. Something from the past that he hasn't come to terms with yet."

"But Fred is so old!" Penelope said. "I'm certain I won't have any new lessons to learn when I'm his age," she added, slipping her hand into her grandpa's.

"I'm not so sure about that, my girl," Grandpa said. But before Penelope could respond, a large swan began nudging the paper bag that Grandpa was holding.

Feeding the ducks wasn't really just feeding the ducks. There were loads of different birds at the lake and they were always Very Hungry. Penelope had only just finished telling Grandpa about Joanna and the drama project when the birds started flocking toward them.

Penelope didn't talk while the birds fed. She just wanted to pause and enjoy the feeling of being in charge of all those birds.

PENELOPE FELT AS THOUGH SHE WAS IN CHARGE OF HER OWN MINI-KINGDOM.

Penelope tried to share out the bread as fairly as possible, but it wasn't easy. Unfortunately, one of the swans was aggressive and behaved very badly. The moorhens were a little better, but Penelope still had to direct her crumbs carefully so everyone got an equal share.

Penelope's favorite bird today was a duck. It had a brown torso and a green neck, which looked lovely. But as well as being lovely to look at, it seemed like a polite and dignified duck. Instead of scrambling for every speck of bread, it accepted the bits that fell in front of it. So it was EXTREMELY annoying when the aggressive swan (for absolutely no reason) gave Penelope's duck a peck on its lovely green neck.

"Just LOOK at that naughty swan," Penelope said to her Grandpa. "It's mucking up everything for all the other birds."

Just as she said that, the naughty swan dived under the water so that only its bottom waggled in front of them. "Truly, it reminds me of Joanna," Penelope said. She looked in the paper bag for some more bread, but it was all gone. The birds must have realized that too, because they started to wander off.

Penelope sighed. Seeing them wandering away gave her the opposite feeling of having the birds flock to her. She and Grandpa George sat on the bench seat. Penelope rested her head on Grandpa's shoulder, watching the aggressive swan finally come the right way up and chase a (very small) moorhen.

"Do you think anyone could train that swan to be GOOD?" Penelope asked.

Grandpa George leaned in so his head rested on top of Penelope's. It was a bit squishy, but Penelope didn't mind.

Grandpa thought for a moment. "I guess it's possible," he said. "But I'm not sure I'd want that to happen."

"Why not?" Penelope asked.

"Well, it's in that swan's nature to behave as it does. And I think it would be boring if everyone behaved the same way."

As much as she loved Grandpa George, Penelope couldn't agree with him on this. You could be different (like Penelope and Bob were different) without being naughty.

Penelope was about to argue that point (although possibly she would need to extract her head before doing it) when Grandpa reached into the pocket of his jacket and pulled out a piece of paper. Penelope eased her head out from under his so she could look at it.

Color outside the lines.
You might be surprised
how good it feels.

Grandpa George often gave Penelope little poems or sayings after he'd checked her astrological chart. Sometimes they were just funny. But every now and then they were really useful.

Penelope smiled. It was nice, in a way, that she would always be Grandpa's little girl, but sometimes he forgot that she was getting quite old. She had been coloring inside the lines without any problem since she was about four years old. She could see no reason to start doing it the wrong way now.

☼ ☼ ☼

Seeing Grandpa had been an excellent idea. That night, Penelope felt calmer. And when she found her play in the special box with the lock and key, she felt almost positive. *Likeable Lucy: The Extremely Popular Girl* was a story of triumph. There was only one part for a boy but Penelope just knew it would be better than anything the other kids would be able to write quickly.

Perhaps it would be okay having Joanna in their group. If both Penelope and Bob were strict with her and made sure she didn't muck around too much, it might be fine. Maybe, together, they could *train* Joanna to do things the right way.

Penelope set the alarm on her iPhone for half an hour earlier than usual. Then she put the piece of paper her Grandpa had given her under her pillow. ⁻Even though it was a bit silly, it was still special, because it was from her lovely grandpa. ⁻

CHAPTER

5

The library was very quiet before school on Thursday morning. Ms. Wong helped Penelope make five copies of her play script. She also helped laminate them in the office. From the office, Penelope could see the booth where she'd spent so many lunchtimes writing the play. In a way, that library booth felt like an old friend. But she was relieved she would only ever go there if she wanted to from now on. Those days were most definitely over.

In drama class, Penelope stood tall (well, as tall as she could—she was still the smallest girl in her year) as she waited for the kids in her group to read through the lovely, laminated scripts.

For a while (probably about six seconds) after everyone had finished reading, nobody in the group spoke. Penelope suspected that they were a bit overwhelmed by how good it was.

Finally, Felix Unger piped up. "This is a girls' play," he said. "I'm not doing a girls' play."

"There's only ONE song in it," Tommy Stratton moaned. "Right at the end."

"Thank God," Joanna chimed in.

"What do you mean by that, Joanna?" Tommy demanded in a cross, loud voice.

"It's not even funny," Felix added.

This was a lot of NEGATIVE comments.

"Well, Felix Unger," Penelope said (a little

snappily), "it's not supposed to be funny because it's not a comedy. It's a DRAMA. Which means it's DRAMATIC. Besides, there *is* a funny bit. Right here."

Penelope pointed to the bit where she had written stage directions for the main character, Likeable Lucy, to pause and wait for the audience to finish laughing.

No one said anything then. It was quite rude how they all looked away.

"Well, it definitely needs some songs or it'll be way boring," Tommy said, breaking into a version of "Popular" from the musical *Wicked*. No ears should have to endure Tommy singing that song, thought Penelope.

"Is someone torturing a cat?" Rita called out from across the room. She said it in her sweetest voice, which is how Penelope knew she was being especially mean.

Tommy stopped singing.

"Keep it down over there, losers," Rita continued. "We're trying to write the last scene of our brilliant play."

So far, Bob hadn't said anything. Penelope was a bit annoyed at how quiet she'd been. She hadn't defended Penelope's play at all. Even though the play was FICTIONAL and not actually about Penelope's life before Bob came to Chelsea Primary, *Likeable Lucy: The Extremely Popular Girl* was close to Penelope's heart.

Penelope gave her very best friend a nudge. That seemed to work. Bob held up her script and waved it around to get everyone's attention.

"All right, dudes," Bob said, "here's the deal. You guys have wasted a lot of time arguing. Now we're behind the other groups. So, here are our options." Bob held out her right hand as though she was weighing an option. It looked heavy. "We could all get together out of school hours and make up a new play. Like, say, this Saturday. Or," Bob continued, holding out her left hand (this one was higher, it was obviously a very light option), "we could get on with Penelope's play right now."

Personally, Penelope would have preferred it if Bob had sold the play on its artistic quality, but she had to admit, the threat of using up a Saturday was a clever one.

"Well," Felix said, "there

is one boy's role. I'll do it if I get to play Simon."

"I don't actually mind playing a girl." Tommy grinned. "Boys played girls' parts all the time in Shakespeare's day. I'll be Nancy."

"That's so true, Tommy," Penelope said. "And it's very mature of you and—"

"As long as I get to sing the song at the end," Tommy interrupted.

Penelope tried not to grimace. Tommy was likely to MASSACRE a huge song like "The Greatest Love of All." She'd planned on using a recording for it. Still, she nodded graciously and only gritted her teeth a little bit.

They were going to do her play after all! As long as Penelope got to play the main character, things would be fine.

"I want to be Likeable Lucy," Joanna said. "She's so full of herself. It's funny."

Penelope choked back a scream. Likeable

Lucy wasn't full of herself! She was kind and caring and creative. In fact (though of course the character was completely fictional), Likeable Lucy shared some of Penelope's own good qualities.

The thought of Joanna getting Penelope's favorite part was bad enough. Penelope couldn't stand the idea of her playing that part for laughs.

Bob must have noticed Penelope's squished-down scream, because she pulled her aside.

"Go with it, Pen," Bob whispered. "Just make sure you call dibs on being the director. That way you get to tell everyone what to do."

Bob gave Penelope a very cheeky grin. "Including Joanna," she added, bumping Penelope on the shoulder.

Penelope breathed in deeply. Perhaps Bob was right. And being the writer *and* director was more important than getting to play Likeable Lucy. She would just explain to Joanna that Lucy was kind and caring and not at all full of herself.

Joanna could hardly argue with the person who CREATED the character. And she certainly couldn't argue with the director, because the director was the boss.

Penelope nodded solemnly. She was (quite) sure that most important play writers and directors would be treated in a more dignified way than she had been.

She had a goal she could not lose sight of. The play would be excellent, and so would her report card at the end of term.

The show must go on.

CHAPTER

On Friday it was quite difficult to be the director because there was no drama class. But Penelope was determined.

SHE HAD TO CONVINCE HER ACTORS TO LEARN THEIR LINES OVER THE WEEKEND.

That night, Penelope sat in her bedroom, script in hand. She tried to ignore the thumping sound coming from Harry's room. Her big brother was OBSESSED with the basketball hoop on his wall.

Opposite Penelope, in his own chair, sat Blue Teddy. Penelope knew that it was a bit silly to have him there. She was (quite) aware that Blue Teddy wasn't actually real. She was also (quite) aware that most girls as grown-up as she was didn't have conversations with their toys anymore.

But Penelope found that Blue Teddy made a good and supportive audience. In fact (if Penelope didn't know better), she could have sworn she saw him lean in toward her so he could concentrate on her play.

Penelope started from the very beginning of the play. It was a big job, but as both director and actor, she thought she should learn EVERYONE'S lines. She knew that actors in real plays had understudies who knew their ENTIRE part and could take over in an emergency. Penelope had a (small) role in the play, and wasn't sure how it would work to play more than one character, but she thought it was a good idea to be prepared.

Penelope was halfway through Likeable Lucy's monologue (the bit where all the other kids in her year had finally realized how kind and caring and creative she actually was, and suddenly she was so in demand at lunchtimes that she had to graciously tell everyone when she would be able to join their activities) when her bedroom door flew open. **Without a single knock!** Very quickly, Penelope grabbed Blue Teddy and put him on her dressing table with zebra and her other toys.

"Are you talking to yourself?" Harry asked, his eyes darting around the room. When Harry's eyes landed on the chair opposite her, she lifted her feet onto it (even though, unlike her mum and brother, Penelope did not think feet and furniture went together).

"Of course not!" Penelope replied. "I'm learning lines for a play we're doing at school next week."

She did not tell Harry she was learning EVERYONE'S lines because that was precisely the kind of thing Harry would NOT understand.

"Ah, okay," Harry replied. "Listen, Mum just texted. She wants me to unpack the dishwasher and you to wipe the benches before she gets home from work. But I want to shoot some more hoops, and you've got to learn your lines. So let's not."

Penelope put down her script. As much

as she would have liked to continue, it was important to remind Harry of the right thing to do. Unfortunately, Harry could be very single-minded.

"Come on, Harry," she said, "let's help Mum."

Penelope worked very hard over the weekend. This was the list she worked through.

> **Penelope Kingston's to-do list**
> 1. Learn everyone's lines!
> 2. Props: basketball, tennis ball, party whistle, masking tape
> 3. Make detailed director's notes to help everyone play their role correctly
> 4. Laminate director's notes

By Sunday afternoon, Penelope had completed the top three tasks.

Unfortunately, Penelope's mother was busy doing chores and said she didn't have time to take her to do the laminating. Which (as Penelope had pointed out) was not actually Very Fair since she had spent at least twenty minutes reading the paper.

Luckily, they were dropping Grandpa George at the airport that evening (he was going on a silent meditation retreat with Fred). So Penelope checked the maps application on her iPhone. There was an office supplies shop that was only a little bit off the highway. They could go on their way home from the airport.

Most NORMAL mothers would be delighted to drive there, happy that their daughter was so hardworking. Not Penelope's mum, though.

Penelope sat in the back seat of the car next to Harry (who had not showered since his soccer game and had mud ALL over him). She leaned forward as far as her seat belt would let her.

"Seriously, Mum," Penelope tried (for the sixth time that day—which just showed how **STUBBORN** and **UNREASONABLE** her mum could be). "It will take half an hour at the most."

"Penelope Kingston," her mum said, glaring at Penelope in the rearview mirror, "I'm putting my foot down. There is absolutely no need for you to laminate your director's notes. You cannot run our family agenda all the time. There will be no visits to office supplies shops this evening. Full stop."

Penelope's hopes were dashed. Her mum hardly ever called her by her full name, but when she did, Penelope knew she would

NEVER get her way (even if she was COMPLETELY in the right).

Penelope bumped back in her seat and crossed her arms.

"Uh-oh," Harry said, "watch out for rain. The little black cloud is back."

"YOU WATCH OUT FOR RAIN, MUD-FACE!" PENELOPE SNAPPED.

"Hey, you two," their mum butted in. "Grandpa George is about to have some precious time away with his friend to meditate and be silent. Perhaps you'd like to kick off the silent bit for us?"

Grandpa George swiveled his head around and winked at them. Penelope kept her arms crossed so he knew she wasn't happy.

"Grandpa," she said after a while, because the silence was already getting boring, "why would you want to go away with Fred and not even be able to talk to him? Why would *anyone* want four whole days of silence?"

"I could think of a reason," Harry said, pointing at Penelope. Which was very rude, especially since her question hadn't been directed at him.

Penelope hardly spoke the rest of the way to the airport.

Just before Grandpa had to go through security, he picked her up. Penelope was (probably) too big to be picked up, but this was a special occasion.

"Sweetheart," he said, giving her a mustache-tickly kiss on the cheek. He looked very thoughtful, like he did when he was reciting a poem or discussing the meaning of dreams. "Fred and I are going on this silent meditation retreat to remind ourselves how to color outside the lines." He paused and put Penelope down.

"I don't think you should ever let yourself get too old for that."

CHAPTER

7

The next time they had drama, Mr. Salmon was wearing red shoes. Perhaps that should have been a warning—Penelope's great plan had started when he'd been wearing green ones. But she was so keen to give everyone her director's notes and props and to see how well they'd learned their lines that she didn't pay much attention.

Mr. Salmon allocated an area of the drama studio for each group to rehearse in. It was noisy, and not as good as having the actual stage to work on, but Penelope was determined to make do. One group was making a human pyramid and another was lining up some chairs in a way that suggested their play was set on a plane. It was a bit disturbing to see Oscar in the same group as (mean) Rita, but Penelope refused to let herself get distracted. She pointed to one of the five crosses she'd made on the floor with masking tape. Even though the crosses wouldn't be there on the actual day of the performance, it was good practice for the actors to work from them.

"You're up first, Bob," she said, pointing to the cross that Bob's character, Bonnie, had to start on. "Action!"

Bonnie: I've made the invitation list for my party. I think I've written down the names of the kids I want to come, but, for some reason, it feels like there's something missing.

"Cut!" Penelope said. "You forgot to say 'all,' Bob. 'I think I've written down *all* the names of the kids I want to come.'"

She pointed to another cross so that Tommy would know where to stand to deliver the next line.

Everything was going really well. Penelope was sure she'd delivered her own lines as Maisie extremely nicely. Next up was Joanna as Likeable Lucy. Penelope crossed her fingers, hoping that Joanna had learned her lines and would be able to deliver them with grace and feeling.

Instead of walking up to the cross, Joanna JUMPED on it. Then she flicked back her hair with both hands in a very SHOWING OFF way, and not at all in the elegant way Penelope had requested in her director's notes. When she delivered her line, her voice was high-pitched and silly.

Likeable Lucy: It's hard being such a deep thinker. Sometimes the other kids don't seem to notice how kind and caring and creative I am. But I have a feeling that things are going to—

"CUT!" Penelope called.

Joanna did seem to know her lines off by heart. But EVERYONE in her group (even Bob!) was laughing. Yes, laughing. Penelope worked to squish down her HORROR. In the past, that sort of feeling had (sometimes, very rarely) meant that the bossy, angry Penelope inside her was about to take over.

Penelope knew she had to be careful. She counted to ten before she spoke.

"Now, Joanna," she said in her Very Patient Explaining Voice. "Likeable Lucy would not flick her hair back with two hands like that." She paused so that Joanna could take in her excellent advice. "Also, she would not talk in that strange voice."

"Chill, Penelope," Felix said. "I reckon Joanna's doing an awesome job. She's funny."

"It's a DRAMA, though, Felix," Penelope reminded him through her teeth. "Joanna, action."

Joanna did a shimmy move that Penelope forced herself to ignore, then continued with her lines.

Likeable Lucy: But I have a feeling that things are about to change. For the better.

Pretty soon, everyone is going to see how kind and creative and caring I am. Because I'm AWESOME.

Penelope felt her nostrils flare. Those last three words weren't even IN THE SCRIPT. Joanna was making her character totally UNlikeable.

IF SHE KEPT GOING LIKE THIS, SHE WAS ABSOLUTELY GOING TO RUIN THE WHOLE PLAY.

Penelope's temples started to throb. She could feel her heart banging against her chest. She had to work Very Hard on taking extra-deep breaths to stop the TYPHOON that was swirling around inside her.

Penelope looked around. Rita Azul was staring at her. Honestly, it seemed as though Rita was destined to witness every one of Penelope's (rare) outbursts. There was actually quite a lot of evidence that Rita could sense them before they even happened. But Penelope was DEFINITELY NOT, UNDER ANY CIRCUMSTANCES, going to give Rita anything new to tease her about.

She took Joanna aside so they could speak privately. It would have been supportive of Bob to come and help Penelope, but Bob was chatting away to Tommy as though Joanna's TREASON was no big deal.

"You need to listen to me, Joanna," Penelope tried to keep her voice calm. It was unfortunate and entirely accidental that a tiny (practically microscopic) bit of spit came out in the hissing part of the word "listen." Anyone else would have let it go. Not Joanna, though.

"Geez, Penelope," Joanna said in a loud voice. She made a great show of wiping her cheek. "Say it, don't spray it. I want the news, not the weather."

It was a Very Bad Moment when Penelope looked over to Rita Azul and saw her laughing and making windshield wiper movements with her hands.

But Penelope was determined to stay calm.

"The thing is, Joanna," Penelope tried again, "that's not how Likeable Lucy would be. She's not vain and silly. She's smart and pretty and kind. You're not doing it the right way. You're using the wrong *character motivation*."

Penelope very much hoped Joanna hadn't been too busy figuring out how to touch her nose with her tongue or shooting pellets out of pen casings or some other naughty thing to pay attention to Mr. Salmon's talk about character motivation. It had been one of his best classes, as far as Penelope was concerned.

Joanna put her hands on her hips in a very UNCOOPERATIVE way.

"It's my choice how I play Likeable Lucy, Penelope," she said. "Stop being so bossy!"

Bossy. Bossy. Bossy.

The terribly unfair accusation landed right in the heart of the TYPHOON inside Penelope and started spinning and whirring until it drowned out her determination to stay calm. Bossy was the LAST thing she was being.

SHE HAD BENT OVER BACKWARD TO LET EVERYONE HAVE THE ROLES THEY WANTED.

She had (graciously) given her group a play she'd written (and laminated!) in her own time. She'd made director's notes and set crosses on the floor and brought along all the props. She had learned all the parts OFF BY HEART.

She was even allowing Tommy Stratton to sing!

BOSSY?

The whirring feelings inside her rose right up to her throat.

There was nothing Penelope could do but open her mouth and let it all spill out.

CHAPTER

8

"I AM NOT BOSSY, JOANNA! NOT EVEN
ONE TINY BIT. WHY SHOULD YOU GET TO
CHOOSE HOW TO PLAY LIKEABLE LUCY
WHEN YOU'RE DOING IT ALL WRONG?
I'M THE DIRECTOR AND I'M THE ONE WHO
MADE HER UP IN THE FIRST PLACE. SHE IS
SUPPOSED TO BE A SERIOUS AND GOOD
AND TRUE PERSON THAT THE OTHER
CHARACTERS LEARN TO LIKE VERY
MUCH. NOT SOME RIDICULOUS PERSON

WHO THINKS THAT GETTING 15/20 FOR A MATH TEST IS FINE, AND SPENDS HALF HER LIFE TRYING TO GET HER TONGUE TO TOUCH HER NOSE."

Penelope was so carried away that she didn't even notice Mr. Salmon's red shoes next to her.

"For goodness' sake, Penelope. You've worked yourself into a state," he said. He pulled up a chair. "Put your head down between your legs and breathe."

Penelope did as Mr. Salmon asked. Five breaths in, she started feeling calmer. After ten breaths though, she began to realize what she'd done. Then she felt like she might just stay like this, with her head down, so she didn't have to face anyone ever again.

She'd done it. She'd had (another) outburst.

Mr. Salmon touched Penelope's shoulder. "Okay, lift your head now," he said. Penelope would never normally disobey a teacher. But she just couldn't do it.

Penelope knew that Joanna was super tough. In fact, the only award Joanna had ever won that wasn't to do with sports (which she was extremely good at) was a resilience award. So she was sure Joanna would just be laughing or rolling her eyes.

But it was possible that the whole class had seen Penelope's outburst. Including (mean) Rita.

The only way Penelope could bring herself to sit up was to visualize her very best friend. Possibly (fingers crossed) the first thing she would see would be Bob, with her special Bob-smile that always made things at least a tiny bit better.

Penelope lifted her head. ⁻And Bob was right there.⁻ Even though she wasn't smiling her Bob-smile, it was still a great relief to see her. It was also a GREAT RELIEF to see that all the other groups (including mean Rita's group) were so busy with their own plays they didn't seem to have noticed Penelope's outburst at all.

BUT IT WAS NOT A RELIEF TO SEE JOANNA.

Because Joanna didn't look resilient. Not at all. She was sitting down (which was already quite un-Joanna-like). Her shoulders were slumped and it looked like her lips were wobbly.

"What happened over here, girls?" Mr. Salmon asked.

Before Penelope could think of a reply, Joanna spoke.

"Nothing," she said. Her voice was soft and not a bit Joanna-ish.

Then, without getting permission from the teacher or organizing for someone to go with her like you were supposed to do, Joanna walked out of the drama studio.

"Go with Joanna, please, Bob," Mr. Salmon said, already walking over to the other side of the studio, where the human pyramid was collapsing.

Penelope looked at her very best friend, expecting Bob to say something comforting about Penelope's rights as a director or perhaps even apologize for not helping pull Joanna into line.

Instead, Bob shook her head. "That was way harsh, Pen," she said.

Then she turned and followed Joanna out of the studio.

◌   ◌   ◌

The lunch bell went very soon after Bob left to find Joanna. As Penelope went to collect her lunch, she held on to her anger. Joanna had pushed her too far this time. She had been terribly rude to insist on playing Likeable Lucy in that silly way. On top of that, she'd called Penelope (the director!) bossy. Which, the more Penelope thought about it, was just ridiculous. The director was *supposed* to be the boss. She was quite keen to point that out to her very best friend.

The locker area was very busy, like it normally was at the start of lunchtime. Practically everyone in Penelope's class was there, opening and closing lockers and getting out lunches.

But one thing was definitely Not Normal.

Bob wasn't there.

Penelope looked around. Every lunchtime since they'd become very best friends (unless one of them was sick) Penelope and Bob got their lunch from the lockers and walked to the bench in the courtyard to eat. Most of the time, they walked from Ms. Pike's classroom together. But if they had separate activities, Penelope and Bob would meet there.

Penelope bit the inside of her lip. She waited for Bob as kids got their lunches and the corridor cleared out.

But Bob didn't show up.

Penelope got her lunchbox out of her locker. Today, as well as her cheese-and-lettuce sandwich and her Pink Lady apple, she had packed two brownies. One for her and one for Bob.

But Bob still wasn't there.

Penelope tried not to think or feel too much as she took her lunch to the bench in the court-yard. Thinking and feeling were probably not going to be good for her right now.

She told herself Bob would be there, on the bench in the courtyard, waiting for her.

For sure.

It was just a matter of putting one foot in front of the other until she got there.

When Penelope arrived at the courtyard, Eliza Chung and Alison Cromwell were there. They were laughing about something. Penelope had no idea what. It was probably a private joke between good friends.

But there was no Bob.

PENELOPE'S LEGS FELT LIKE ROBOT LEGS AS SHE WALKED AROUND THE SCHOOL YARD.

Rita and Sarah were in the playground area with a few other kids. Rita was wobbling the wobbly bridge while Sarah tried to get across. That was pretty much how Rita was all the time. She loved making other people feel wobbly. Penelope was not (even a tiny bit) tempted to join them.

But there was no Bob.

Penelope felt more and more robotlike as she went to check the oval. She hadn't spent a (single) lunchtime alone since Bob became her very best friend. The idea of that happening again was something she TOTALLY didn't want to think about.

Even if she just found Oscar looking at bugs under a magnifying glass she would (probably, even though he was a boy) join him!

But Oscar was playing handball with Felix Unger. And there was still no Bob.

PENELOPE FELT COMPLETELY MECHANICAL NOW.

She walked up the stairs to the library. By herself.

She snuck into her favorite booth. It was a very nice booth with a window and not too much rude graffiti. The same very nice booth where she'd sat by herself at lunch-times, writing *Likeable Lucy: The Extremely Popular Girl*.

Before she had her very own best friend.

Through the window, Penelope could see the courtyard and the oval. In the court-yard, Alison was braiding Eliza's hair. A game of dodgeball was beginning on the oval. Penelope was not a fan of dodgeball. But the shouts and laughter rising up from the game made her feel like she was missing out on something.

Again.

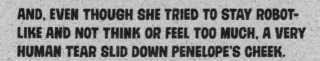

AND, EVEN THOUGH SHE TRIED TO STAY ROBOT-LIKE AND NOT THINK OR FEEL TOO MUCH, A VERY HUMAN TEAR SLID DOWN PENELOPE'S CHEEK.

Penelope knew that the lunch break had been the normal length (50 minutes, 1:15 p.m.–2:05 p.m.). But this lunch break seemed to stretch out much longer. In the olden days (before she had her own very best friend) Penelope hadn't minded staying in the library. (It was a very nice library booth.)

Now, though, things were different. Penelope could never (not ever) go back to spending her lunchtimes there.

So, after lunch, when Bob (finally) walked into class with Joanna, Penelope smiled at both of them so they would know she was ready to patch things up. Joanna poked out her tongue, but that was pretty normal for Joanna. Penelope was relieved to see that Joanna seemed okay.

"Where were you at lunchtime, Bob?" Penelope asked brightly as her very best friend (which she still was!) sat down next to her. "You didn't show up at the courtyard and I looked for you everywhere."

Bob looked at Penelope. There was no Bob-smile.

"Mostly in the restroom with Joanna," Bob said. Her voice sounded cold. "She was pretty cut up by what you said."

Penelope had a sinking feeling in her chest.

"Ah, but—" she began. "I just got cross because Joanna wasn't playing Likeable Lucy the right way. *We* were going to pull her into line, Bob. Don't you remember?"

Bob sighed.

"You weren't just cross, Pen," she said. "You chucked it. And you were really mean."

Penelope gulped. This was certainly

NOT what she wanted to hear from her very best friend. But Bob wasn't finished.

"And I didn't want to pull Joanna into line because I thought she was doing a good job," Bob continued.

She waited for a moment, but Penelope couldn't think of anything to say.

"Just because people aren't doing things your way, Pen," Bob said finally, "that doesn't mean they're not doing it right."

CHAPTER

That night, as Penelope got ready for bed, she had some very complicated emotions.

She felt sorry that she'd hurt Joanna's feelings. Even though Joanna was naughty and not good at taking direction, she was never mean.

But she also felt worried that she was losing control over her lovely play. It was absolutely possible that Joanna might sink the play completely. Then Penelope would NEVER get to make up for her Truly Terrible Mistake.

It was very bad timing that Grandpa George was away on his silent meditation retreat. Penelope wasn't even allowed to text him. She knew that it was possible to phone the retreat in an emergency. But, even though this was actually a kind of emergency, Penelope didn't want to interrupt his trip.

As Penelope took Blue Teddy off her pillow and climbed into bed, lying nose-to-nose with him, she saw the edge of the astrology note Grandpa George had given her. She reached for her iPhone and switched on the flashlight app so she could read it.

> Color outside the lines.
> You might be surprised
> how good it feels.

If her grandpa had been home, Penelope would have texted him to ask what that actually meant. But, since Grandpa was away, Penelope typed the first four words into Google on her iPhone. Then she tapped Images.

A lot of things came up. But there were two images in particular that were interesting. The first was just writing.

> You have to color outside the lines once in a while to make your life a masterpiece.

The second had a picture of pencils (sharpened and sitting points-up in a mug just like Penelope's own).

> Sometimes you have to see people as pencils. They may not be your favorite color, but you need them to complete the picture.

Penelope still wasn't quite sure she understood what all that meant. But she decided, right there and then, SPONTANEOUSLY, to try Grandpa's advice.

She got out of bed, switched on the light, and walked over to her bookcase. At the moment, her books were arranged in alphabetical order according to the author's surname. Since her old coloring books had no actual author, she'd put them in with the Cs.

Penelope pulled out the one that had been her favorite the year she turned four. It had been a year of big changes. When Penelope was three, her dad still lived with them. By the time she was four, he didn't live with them anymore. But he had sent her the coloring book for her birthday.

The pages were filled with peaceful scenes of houses, rainbows, birds, and hills. Penelope had colored them in with her beloved Derwent pencils. Every sky in the book was done in the same shade (Spectrum Blue). Every cloud was the same shade (Chinese White). Every patch of grass was the same shade (Grass Green).

Penelope looked at each picture. Page after page. Even though it had been a long time since she'd worked on this coloring book, she remembered how much care and effort she'd put into getting everything exactly right. There was not a single place where she'd gone outside the lines.

She also remembered what she'd told herself while she was putting in all that time and effort. That if she did an excellent job, and there was not a single bit of color outside any of the lines, her dad would come back to live with them.

That had been a crazy thing to

tell herself. And perhaps even four-year-old Penelope hadn't believed it. Because on the very last page of the coloring book was a picture of a lovely cottage in the forest.

And it was not colored in. At all.

At first, she had to force herself to do it.

For the sky, she used Orange Chrome. When she held the picture out at arm's length, Penelope was surprised to find that she didn't mind it.

For the trees in the forest, Penelope chose Imperial Purple. Then she added extra branches that were completely *out of the lines*. As she chose a color for the tree trunk (Rose Pink), Penelope thought about Joanna's approach to playing Likeable Lucy. Obviously it wasn't what Penelope had imagined when she created the character, but maybe that wasn't *such* a bad thing. Perhaps it was a bit like having an orange sky. Or purple trees with pink trunks.

As she worked on the sun (Emerald Green), Penelope thought about Joanna as Likeable Lucy, jumping onto the cross on the floor and

AND, INSTEAD OF BEING ANGRY ABOUT IT, SHE ACTUALLY SMILED.

flicking her hair back with both hands.

Bob was right. Penelope had been too harsh. If she could take back what she'd said to Joanna, she'd do it right away.

Penelope breathed deeply as she looked at her finished picture. It *should* look terrible and all wrong, but it actually looked sort of lovely in its own (slightly weird) way. Maybe it wasn't a masterpiece. But it did make the other pictures seem a bit boring.

Maybe things could be different from the way you thought they should be, but still work out somehow. . . .

Really, it would have been nice if Grandpa's astrology note had been a little more to the point, rather than leaving Penelope to discover the meaning behind it.

Perhaps she should let Joanna do things her own way, even if it didn't seem correct to

Penelope. Was it possible that Joanna could make the play *better*?

Penelope couldn't unsay what she'd said to Joanna.

— But she could try to fix things. —

CHAPTER

First up the next day was PE. Penelope did not love PE. She especially did not love PE when Mr. Joseph made them go for a (very long) cross-country run. But today, Penelope had a plan.

Joanna was always way better behaved when she was doing something sporty. Very long cross-country runs seemed to calm her down and make her more sensible. Joanna had won several awards for cross-country.

It would take effort and energy and perhaps all the puff Penelope had, but she was going to stick beside Joanna on the run. At least until they'd talked about getting the play back on track.

"All right, troops," Mr. Joseph said as they assembled at the gym.

When everyone was paying attention, Mr. Joseph fired the starting gun (even though it was absolutely unnecessary, and he could have just used his voice so no one got a fright).

Penelope started strongly. She moved through the runners until she was side by side with Joanna.

"Joanna," she puffed, "I wanted to talk to you about that drama class."

It was very difficult to keep up. Penelope had to take two steps to every one of Joanna's. But she was determined to sort this out.

"I'm," she puffed, "sorry if I . . . ," puff, "hurt . . . ," puff, puff, "your feelings, Joanna."

"It's all right, Penelope," Joanna said, without a single puff in her voice, as though a (very long) cross-country run was easy peasy. "I'm over it now. I'm pretty used to it anyway. People are always telling me I'm stupid."

That made Penelope's tummy feel tense. She normally tried to make people feel ‑BETTER‑ about themselves, not WORSE (except when she was having an outburst and things sometimes came out quite wrong and a teensy bit mean).

Admittedly, Joanna did put effort and energy into odd things. The tongue-touching-the-nose thing was a very good example of this. But Penelope thought Joanna was quite clever when she focused properly.

Having a tense tummy, though, was not ideal when it was combined with feeling EXTREMELY puffed out. It was difficult for Penelope to explain things to Joanna while she was panting. Penelope had to stop then, as she was doubled over with a stitch.

"OMG, Penelope," Joanna said, stopping too. "You went too fast too early. You're supposed to pace yourself with cross-country. You look like you're going to throw up."

Joanna looked around in the way Penelope had witnessed many times before. It was the look she had whenever she was about to do something naughty.

Only a couple of meters away was the biggest tree in the whole school. It had strong branches and a very dense canopy. Penelope knew it was naughty to hide in there, but she was too puffed to protest when Joanna lifted a leafy branch and led her into the famous Chelsea Primary hiding place. Lots of other kids used the tree to hide from the teachers during class (which Penelope knew was Very Wrong).

Penelope had seen the space before, but she'd never actually been inside. She had to duck her head to get in, but once she had done so, the space opened up.

Joanna steered Penelope over to a sort of natural bench made by the roots of the tree. Penelope sat down to recover her breath.

In any other circumstances, Penelope would have got out of there as quickly as possible. But she glanced up and there, stuck on the tree trunk, was the (laminated) script from the play!

"I've been sneaking in here whenever I can," Joanna explained. "Learning my lines."

"EVEN AT RECESS AND LUNCHTIME."

Penelope heard the thumping sound of runners passing the tree. ⁻It was very kind of Joanna to stay with her. ⁻ Being in here would most likely mean that Joanna wouldn't even finish the run—let alone win it. Part of Penelope wanted to push her out so she could get back into the race.

But even though Penelope had recovered her breath, and even though hiding there was definitely naughty and they should both get back out there so Joanna could go and win the race, Penelope didn't want to leave. Not yet.

"Joanna," she said, shaking her head, "that is very dedicated." It seemed that she had really underestimated Joanna this time.

"Listen," she said, "I need to try to explain why I got so worked up about how you were playing Likeable Lucy. It's a very complicated thing and it will probably be hard for you to understand."

"Hang on," Joanna said. She reached inside a hole in the tree and pulled out a giant stick of bubble gum. This gave Penelope a pretty good clue about how the script was staying stuck. "Want some?" Joanna asked.

Penelope shook her head. Just being in there, skipping the race, was naughty enough for her.

"Right, go on," Joanna said, shoving a piece of bubble gum in her mouth.

"Way back, a long time ago when I wrote the play," Penelope began, "things weren't going so well for me at school."

She paused while Joanna reached over and grabbed a drink bottle from her stash in the tree. "At least," she continued, "*some* things weren't going so well."

Penelope paused again. Finding the right words was difficult.

Joanna blew a bubble that was possibly one of the largest Penelope had ever seen. It was definitely the largest she'd ever seen on school grounds (where bubble gum was totally not allowed).

"I reckon I get it," Joanna said, pushing the lump of gum to one side so that it bulged inside her cheek. "Before Bob came to Chelsea Primary, you were lonely. So you made up this character called Likeable Lucy, who was lonely but then became super popular. Someone who does things her own way, but triumphs in the end. That's the whole deal about the song at the end, right? 'The Greatest Love of All' is about learning to love yourself."

Penelope was stunned. Doubly stunned, actually. She was stunned by Joanna fishing the bubble gum out of her mouth and stuffing it back into the packet.

But she was more stunned by Joanna's Very Deep Thoughts. That Joanna even had Very Deep Thoughts made Penelope feel much better about letting her play Likeable Lucy her way.

"You do realize that the characters are entirely fictional?" she asked, just to be sure.

"Er, yeah," Joanna said. "Obviously picking up a little kid who's fallen down in the playground isn't going to make anyone crazy popular in real life. And geez, even Ellen Semorac isn't as popular as Likeable Lucy, and she's the most popular girl in the whole school."

Penelope wasn't quite sure she agreed with that. She actually thought that helping a kid who'd fallen down in the playground could be a great way to become popular (maybe if the whole school could somehow witness the good deed). It just so happened that she had an award at home called "The Watchful Eye" for performing exactly that good deed. She had to admit, however, that it hadn't improved her popularity.

But there was no need to argue about it. She'd made her decision.

"Joanna," she said, "you have my permission, as director, to play Likeable Lucy however you want," Penelope said.

"Cool," Joanna said, taking one last swig from her drink bottle, "'cause I was going to do it my way anyway."

Penelope decided not to react to that comment, either. She lifted the tree canopy to peek outside, then turned back to Joanna.

"Thanks for looking after me," she said. "I know you could have won the race."

Joanna shrugged as though it was no big deal.

"And," Penelope continued, "you are absolutely NOT stupid."

‾As soon as she said that, Penelope felt lighter. ‾ In fact (and this was very weird), even though it was clearly naughty to be hiding in the middle of a cross-country race, somehow, suddenly, it felt okay.

"Thanks for that," Joanna said. "And hey, check this out."

For a second, Penelope wondered if Joanna was going to give her another deep thought.

INSTEAD (VERY CONVINCINGLY AND WITHOUT ANY GAP AT ALL), JOANNA TOUCHED HER NOSE WITH HER TONGUE.

CHAPTER

11

It was Thursday. The day of the Big Performance. Penelope had set her harp alarm so she could get up early and brush up on everyone's lines. But it was actually the beep of an incoming text message that woke her up. It was from Grandpa George.

> On our way home from the retreat. It was terrific. I figured out a lot about myself. And Fred realized he was being weighed down by an old grudge. He's decided to let the grudge

> go, and now his flying dreams are wonderful again. I hope you've been coloring outside the lines, sweetheart. Good luck today. I'll be thinking of you. G x

Penelope took a deep breath. Obviously Fred wasn't too old to learn new lessons after all. ¯She was very glad for him.¯ Penelope hoped that things would go well for her, too.

Mr. Salmon had transformed the drama studio for performance day. The windows were covered with black cardboard, making it very dark, and the lights around the stage were dazzling.

"Woo hoo!" Bob said, giving Penelope a (friendly) pinch on the thigh as they sat cross-legged on the floor. "I'm so pumped. This is crazy cool, hey, Pen?"

‑Penelope returned the pinch. ‑ It was good to know that their friendship was totally back on track now she'd sorted things out with Joanna. But Penelope felt very nervous about the play. After all, she was the writer *and* director, so the success of *Likeable Lucy: The Extremely Popular Girl* really rested on her shoulders.

"Ladies and gentlemen, boys and girls," Mr. Salmon said in a grand theatrical voice, "I've been so pleased to see you all working hard on your plays. It's a great challenge, as it involves both creativity and cooperation. I'm certainly hoping for some quality performances this afternoon. So, without further ado, I give you . . ." He shuffled some papers in his hands, and then adjusted the lighting, which actually WAS a bit of further ado, Penelope thought. "I give you *Murder on the Train!*"

Then there was even more ado while Alison Cromwell's group set up chairs onstage. Penelope was always very interested in what Alison did because she was excellent at a lot of things (like Penelope).

At Chelsea Primary, awards were given every Friday at assembly. Penelope (who now had 51 awards) was still leading. But Alison was getting scarily close with 39 awards.

Alison's group's play was about a murderer on a train (not a plane, as Penelope had originally thought). It was definitely an entertaining play, and the bit where Sarah cut Alison's throat and her (fake) head fell off was gripping. The downfall, as far as Penelope was concerned, was at the end when all the dead bodies were jiggling up and down in a way that suggested they were laughing (which of course dead bodies do not do).

Mr. Salmon held up his score card, and everyone cheered. He had given the group 8/10.

The next group's play was called *Stacking Up*. Given that Eliza Chung (Class Captain!) was in this group, Penelope expected the play to be a bit better than it was. The only proper, scripted bit was at the beginning when the characters started arguing about who was the strongest. The rest was pretty much just about forming a human pyramid. If Penelope had been the judge she would have given them points for an impressive human pyramid. Then she would have taken points away for all the groaning the kids at the bottom of the pyramid did.

Mr. Salmon seemed to agree with Penelope's point of view, because he gave *Stacking Up* 7/10.

After that came Oscar and Rita's group. Their play was called *Timeless*. It was about a group of young friends who were playing around with a frisbee they had found at the park. It turned out that they followed the frisbee into another time zone. The way they did this was very creative. It involved each character following the frisbee behind the curtain and offstage. When the characters came back onstage, they were now old.

Penelope had to admit that Rita was pretty good at playing a grumpy old lady.

BUT OSCAR WAS THE STANDOUT.

He came back onstage wearing glasses and a long, gray beard, and made his voice sound old by adding a tremor to it.

The audience had applauded at the end of each play, but when Oscar took his bow, there was hooting as well. _ Even Penelope hooted (though she covered her mouth so it wasn't too loud). _

Mr. Salmon's score was very high. Possibly even unbeatable. 9/10.

Then (finally!) Mr. Salmon introduced Penelope's group.

☽ ☾ ☽

Penelope had NEVER enjoyed performing so much (not even when she'd played one of the mice in *Cinderella*). She was nervous—butterflies definitely flapped their wings inside her chest (not literally—Penelope would never actually swallow a butterfly!). But right from the beginning of the play, she just had a feeling that things were going to work.

–And they did.–

The audience went MAD for Likeable Lucy. In fact, Sarah and Tilly laughed so hard that they smacked their heads together! But there were some tender moments as well, when the audience stayed quiet and listened.

It was a Very Weird thing. Originally, Penelope's play had been a drama. But Penelope could see, now, that if she'd played Likeable Lucy in the way she'd planned, the whole thing might have just been sad—and even a little bit dull.

Joanna's Likeable Lucy was very funny. But her being funny didn't make the play any less important. It seemed to draw the audience closer, so that when they got to the serious bits, everyone leaned in and listened.

By the end, Penelope wished they could go back and do the whole thing again.

The audience clapped enthusiastically. Joanna took her bow, and they hooted and hollered. Then, standing all in a row, they took a group bow.

PENELOPE WAS DELIGHTED TO HAVE BOB ON HER LEFT AND JOANNA ON HER RIGHT.

She held her breath as Mr. Salmon revealed their score. 9.5/10! This was, most likely, the highest score he had EVER given.

They stayed onstage while Tommy Stratton launched into his version of "The Greatest Love of All." Penelope decided it was okay that they hadn't used a recording like she had planned. And, if everyone formed a stampede to get out of the drama studio as soon as the bell went (even though Tommy hadn't even reached the chorus) that was okay too.

So many things had gone WRONG with this project.

─ But somehow the wrong things had all added up to make things totally RIGHT. ─

ABOUT THE AUTHOR

Chrissie Perry is the author of more than thirty books for children and young adults, including thirteen books in the popular Go Girl series and the award-winning *Whisper*. She lives in St. Kilda, Australia, with her husband and three children.

Like Penelope Kingston, Chrissie believes it's great to aim for excellence. But she also has a sneaking suspicion that going with the flow every now and then can also work out just fine.

Looking for another great book?
Find it
IN THE MIDDLE.

Fun, fantastic books for kids
in the in-beTWEEN age.

IntheMiddleBooks.com

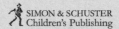

The perfect beginning . . . almost.

Penelope is going to camp—

and this year it will be perfect. . . .

It's time for the school fair, and Penelope is running a booth—and it's going to be just perfect. . . .